Yang the Eldest and His Odd Jobs

Yang the Eldest and His Odd Jobs

Lensey Namioka

Illustrated by Kees de Kiefte

Little, Brown and Company
Boston New York London

First Edition

The characters and events portrayed in this book are fictitious. Any similarity to real persons, living or dead, is coincidental and not intended by the author.

Library of Congress Cataloging-in-Publication Data

Namioka, Lensey.
    Yang the eldest and his odd jobs / Lensey Namioka ;
illustrated by Kees de Kiefte. — 1st ed.
        p.   cm.
    Summary: Third Sister and her siblings try to help Eldest Brother, the most talented musician in the Yang family, find work to pay for a new violin.
    ISBN 0-316-59011-8
    1. Chinese Americans — Juvenile fiction. [1. Chinese Americans — Fiction. 2. Moneymaking projects — Fiction. 3. Violin — Fiction. 4. Musicians — Fiction. 5. Brothers and sisters — Fiction.]
    I. Kiefte, Kees de, ill.   II. Title.
    PZ7.N1426Yaf   2000
    [Fic] — dc21   99-36935

10 9 8 7 6 5 4 3 2 1

MV-NY

Printed in the United States of America

To the musicians:
Aki, Diana, Erik, Marilyn, Michi,
Noreen, Sandra, Sara, Steven
— L. N.

To Lensey
— K. de K.

Yang the Eldest and His Odd Jobs

1

"It keeps buzzing," Eldest Brother said, and stopped playing.

He was the first violinist and our leader, so the rest of us all stopped, too. In our quartet, Matthew Conner plays the second violin and Second Sister plays the viola. I'm the Third Sister in our family, and I play the cello. Fourth Brother has such a terrible ear that his friend Matthew replaced him as second violin. Now he plays baseball instead, and we're all very happy about that.

Eldest Brother put his ear to the body of his instrument and plucked at the E-string. He frowned at what he was hearing.

"What's buzzing?" asked Second Sister. "Is it caused by the bow? Maybe you need more rosin."

Eldest Brother looked worried. "No, the buzzing comes from something inside the body."

"Maybe some bug is trapped in there," suggested Matthew.

"I bet it's a bee," I said. Seeing that Eldest Brother looked worried, I tried to make a joke. "Too bad you aren't a pianist, or you could play 'Flight of the Bumblebee.'"

Nobody smiled at my feeble joke, and we went back to our music. But Eldest Brother was distracted and played badly, which was very unusual for him. Finally Second Sister shook her head. "It's no use playing if you can't concentrate, Eldest Brother. You'd better get Mr. Vitelli to check out your violin."

Next morning, Eldest Brother and I took the bus to Mr. Vitelli's shop in the Capitol Hill area of Seattle. The neighborhood is full of huge, old houses that once belonged to families with lots of children. Nowadays families tend to be smaller, and many of the houses there have been divided for more than one household. Others are being used as schools or for businesses. Mr. Vitelli's violin shop occupies a big three-story house full of gables, towers, and windows in unexpected places.

I wish our family could afford to move into a house like that. Right now, we live in only half a house and share the other half with an elderly couple called the Sylvesters. Still, this is a lot more room than we used to have in Shanghai, where we lived in a two-bedroom apartment and shared a bathroom with four other families!

I went along to Mr. Vitelli's with Eldest Brother because I always love visiting his shop. The place is full of fascinating instruments, some of them really ancient. Also, it's easy to get Mr. Vitelli started telling stories about the musicians and instruments he has encountered over the years. I don't know how old he is. He's a small man and very wrinkled, like a dehydrated elf. But when he talked about meeting Paganini, who lived two hundred years ago, I knew he was kidding — even before seeing the twinkle in his eye.

When Eldest Brother brought out his violin, however, Mr. Vitelli's eyes were not twinkling. He examined every part of the instrument very carefully, then picked up the bow and played a few notes. His fingers were thick, but they had a delicate touch.

"The buzzing sound in your violin could be caused by a number of things," he finally said.

His face looked grave, and I suspected that he was going to give us bad news.

I was right. "My guess is that the sound bar is loose and needs to be reglued," Mr. Vitelli continued. "Or it could be something else that's come loose. Whatever it is, I'm afraid I'll have to take the top off and look inside."

I knew that taking the top off a violin was a serious operation — like cutting open someone's stomach to look at his insides. "How much will the repair cost?" Eldest Brother asked.

"Taking the top off and fixing the sound bar would cost at least four or five hundred dollars," said Mr. Vitelli, looking apologetic. "It's the labor, you see."

"I don't think my father paid that much when he bought my violin," Eldest Brother said with a sigh. We had all brought our instruments over from China, where labor was a lot cheaper.

Mr. Vitelli is one of the best violin makers in town. My father and brother trust him completely and always go to him whenever they need any work done. If he said he had to take the top off the violin to fix it, it was unavoidable.

Eldest Brother sighed again. "I guess I'll just have to rent a violin until I decide what to do next."

He didn't say so, but we both knew what he had to do next: buy a *new* violin. But where would he find the money? A decent violin costs a few hundred dollars in China, but here in America a good one costs about ten times that much. Maybe you can buy one in installments. I had heard that you can buy a car or a house in installments, so why not a violin?

Naturally we couldn't resist looking at the instruments in Mr. Vitelli's shop. Some of them were for sale, and some were there to be repaired. I was fascinated by a tiny violin, one-sixteenth size, about right for a toddler. The player would have to be a child prodigy. I guess some parents never give up hope of producing another young Mozart.

Suddenly there was a gasp from Eldest Brother. "Is this for sale?"

Mr. Vitelli picked up the violin that Eldest Brother was looking at. "I just finished making that last month. It's the best work I've done in years — maybe the best work I've *ever* done. So far I haven't had the heart to put a price on it." He held out the violin. "Do you want to try it?"

Eldest Brother received the instrument with awe, plucked the strings to check the tuning, and picked up the bow. Then he closed his eyes

and began to play. The music was so piercingly sweet that my throat ached and tears came into my eyes.

Eldest Brother stopped playing abruptly. As he put the violin down on the counter, it almost seemed to stick to his hands. Then the silence was broken as the front door of the shop opened with a jingling of bells.

Mr. Vitelli cleared his throat. "I guess I'd better attend to my customer."

Eldest Brother muttered his thanks to Mr. Vitelli, took one last lingering look at the shining violin he had just played, picked up his own battered violin case, and went to the door. I followed him out of the store.

We walked to the bus stop without saying anything. Just as our bus arrived, I heard Eldest Brother say softly, "I'd do anything — anything — to buy that violin!"

At supper that evening, the talk around the table was mostly about Eldest Brother's violin. Father looked dismayed when he heard what Mr. Vitelli had said about having to remove the top of the violin to get at the buzzing problem. "That sounds serious," he said.

I tried to be cheerful. "Maybe nobody will

notice the buzzing, Eldest Brother. Not everybody can hear as well as you do."

"But *I* can hear it," said Eldest Brother. "And that disturbs my playing. Besides, if the sound bar is loose, as Mr. Vitelli suspects, the problem will only get worse and worse."

"The violin may not be worth the cost of the repair," sighed Father. "We'll have to think about getting a new instrument."

"I saw a beautiful new violin in Mr. Vitelli's shop today," Eldest Brother said dreamily. I could hear the yearning in his voice.

Father looked sharply at him. "How much is he asking for it?"

Eldest Brother came down to earth with a thump. After a moment he said, "He didn't say, but I'm sure it will be very expensive. It may be the best thing he's ever made, he said."

For a while nobody said anything as we continued eating. But the same thought must have been on everyone's mind: money. We're better off now than when we first arrived in America from China. Father started as a substitute player in the Seattle Symphony, but he is now a full member of the orchestra and draws a regular salary. He is also getting more music students.

But that doesn't mean he's rolling in money. Mother was a professional pianist in China and had a job as an accompanist. But she has not found work since coming to America.

Second Sister and I both earn money baby-sitting. Fourth Brother makes some money helping his friend Matthew deliver newspapers. He doesn't earn much that way, but he doesn't spend much, either.

Eldest Brother is the only one in the family who hasn't done anything to earn money. We've all known that among the Yangs, he is the most gifted musically, and it just seems natural that he should spend every free minute practicing. He is totally dedicated to music.

"In China, the government would provide an instrument for a musician as good as Eldest Brother," said Second Sister. "Why don't Americans do more to support talented people?"

Second Sister is the one who misses China most, so she is also the one who is quickest to criticize America. But I knew what she meant. The Chinese government runs schools for musicians, athletes, even acrobats, who show a special talent. If our family had stayed in China, Eldest Brother would be going to a music school right now. Everything would be provided for him: room, board, tuition, and a high-quality instrument.

"Why did we leave China, anyway?" muttered Second Sister.

I saw my parents look at each other. Immigrating to America had not been an easy step, and they had done their best to explain their decision to us.

When Eldest Brother was born, my parents were thrilled. Almost immediately he showed an unusual gift for music. Even before he was one, he could repeat a tune perfectly on pitch when Mother sang to him. My parents were so delighted with their infant prodigy that they decided to have another baby. In China, a couple is supposed to have only one child, in order to control the population growth. But my parents felt that in the end they were doing a good thing for their country by contributing to the supply of musical talent.

Their next baby turned out to be Second Sister, who was also talented musically. Then I was born, also with a good ear for music. Why stop when they were ahead? At that rate, thought Father, he would produce his very own string quartet. Maybe he had become a little too vain,

12

and his luck ran out when Fourth Brother was born with a terrible ear.

My parents were harshly criticized for having more than one child. With each additional baby, their life became harder. We were refused permission to move to a larger apartment. When my parents complained that families with only three people had far more room than our family of six, they were told that it was their own fault for having so many children.

Again and again, Father was passed over for promotion in the orchestra, and he had to watch violinists far inferior to him get higher chairs. Nor did he get the raises or the bonuses received by the other players. Mother lost her job as an accompanist, and most of her piano students stopped coming to her for lessons.

Then, Father met an American conductor who was touring China with his orchestra. The conductor was able to find a sponsor willing to help our family immigrate to this country. Except for Second Sister, we are all very happy that we have made it here. And even Second Sister has her happy moments, too.

But I had to admit that the state-run music schools in China would have made things easier for Eldest Brother. As my friend Kim explained,

America operates under a market economy. That means you can't expect anybody to support you unless you have something they want to buy. If you want to be a musician, you have to earn your own way.

"Eldest Brother will just have to earn some money if he wants to buy Mr. Vitelli's violin," I said, thinking aloud.

The rest of my family stared at me. I took a deep breath. "Eldest Brother has to go out and get a job."

2

It was summer vacation, so Eldest Brother would have plenty of time to get a job. But what could he do? The first thing I did the next day was call up my friend Kim for ideas.

"Hi, Mary, what's up?" asked Kim. My Chinese name is Yingmei, but I knew my American friends would have a hard time remembering it, so I gave myself the English name of Mary.

"Is Jason around?" I asked. "My eldest brother needs to earn some money for a new violin, and I was wondering if Jason could help him get a summer job."

Jason is in the same grade as Eldest Brother. They aren't close like Kim and me, but they're more friendly than they used to be.

"Jason's gone for the rest of the summer," said Kim. "He just got a job as a counselor at a

15

soccer camp. It doesn't pay much, but he likes it. We got a card from him yesterday, and he says some of the younger kids can be a handful."

I'm always surprised by all the different sorts of camps that kids in America can go to during summer vacation. In fact, Kim and I went to a music camp last month, and I had the best time of my life during our two weeks there. The camp counselors were teenagers only a few years older than we are. During breaks from the music, they took us swimming, hiking, and even fishing. In the evening, we sat around the campfire singing silly songs. After playing classical music most of the day, we enjoyed singing something zany for a change.

"Hey, maybe your brother can be a counselor at a music camp," suggested Kim. "The camp directors would be glad to get someone as good as he is."

Eldest Brother might be a good musician, but could he handle a bunch of noisy little kids? "Frankly, I have a hard time picturing Eldest Brother fishing or singing silly songs," I said.

"It's probably too late for him to apply for this

summer, anyway," said Kim. "How about next summer?"

The trouble was that Eldest Brother couldn't wait until next summer. The sound bar in his violin might become too loose for him to continue playing it, and Mr. Vitelli's beautiful instrument would probably be sold before then.

How could Eldest Brother start earning some money right away? Suddenly, I had an idea. *I* earned money by baby-sitting. Maybe Eldest Brother could do some baby-sitting, too! I had a job lined up for the coming weekend, but since I didn't need the money so much, I could let Eldest Brother take my place.

After supper, I stopped Eldest Brother before he could go upstairs to practice. "Can I talk to you for a minute?"

Normally, only an alien invasion could stop Eldest Brother from practicing. But ever since the buzzing started in his violin, he had become less keen on playing. He stopped with one foot on the staircase. "What is it, Third Sister?"

I cleared my throat. "It's about finding a job for you."

"You really think I can earn enough money to buy Mr. Vitelli's violin?" he asked, surprised.

"This is America," I said, "the land of opportunity. People make their own way in this country." I've got all sorts of useful English phrases written down in a notebook, and I especially like the sound of "land of opportunity" and "people make their own way."

"But what can I do?" asked Eldest Brother. "Father is much more experienced than I am, but even he doesn't earn enough to walk into Mr. Vitelli's shop and pay thousands of dollars for that new violin."

"I earned enough by baby-sitting to pay for my music camp," I told him.

"That's true, you did," he said slowly. "So you think I should try baby-sitting?"

"I'm supposed to sit Peter Schultz and his sister this Saturday," I said. "I can ask Mrs. Schultz if she'll let you take my place."

Peter Schultz is one of Father's violin students, and at age five, he is the youngest. Both Second Sister and I have sat the Schultz kids lots of times.

When I called Mrs. Schultz to suggest Eldest Brother substituting for me, she sounded hesitant. "Does he have any experience?" she asked.

I paused. "Well, not exactly," I said. "But he helped take care of all of us Yangs when we were little."

"Hmmm . . ." Mrs. Schultz still seemed reluctant. I had to think of something fast. "Plus, he could help Peter practice his violin!" I said brightly.

That did it. Mrs. Schultz sounded almost eager when she accepted Eldest Brother as a sitter.

After hanging up, I suddenly began to feel a bit uneasy. I still remember how scary it was the first time I went out on a baby-sitting job. Second Sister had done it already, and she helped me a lot by telling me what to expect. In fact, she practically gave me a whole lecture on baby-sitting. Now I had to do the same for Eldest Brother.

On Saturday afternoon, I approached Eldest Brother and suggested having a little talk about what to expect at the Schultzes'. It felt funny to sit down with Eldest Brother and give him advice on baby-sitting. He's the person I admire most in the world, and all my life I've been used to listening to *him* lecture *me* on what to do.

In a Chinese family, we're supposed to be respectful toward our elders. I'm always shocked when I hear my friend Kim bossing her brother around. "Why shouldn't I?" demanded Kim. "I know more than Jason does about a lot of things!"

I like this American attitude, but I've been brought up differently, and I just can't bring myself to act like Kim. It would have been a little better for Second Sister to advise Eldest Brother. At least she's closer to him in age.

But Second Sister was busy Saturday night. She was going to a movie with Paul Eng — who was *not* a boyfriend, according to her. She also insisted that this was *not* a date, and that they were just going together because both of them love kung fu movies. None of us contradicted her. We all nodded solemnly and said, "Yes, yes, of course, we understand."

So I was the one who had to give Eldest Brother a lesson in baby-sitting. Sitting across from him at the kitchen table, I tried to think where I should start. "Uh, I'd better begin with diapers," I said.

Eldest Brother's eyes widened. "Peter is five years old! You mean American kids still aren't toilet trained as late as that?"

"No, it's his younger sister, Carrie, who is still in diapers," I told him. "She's only one and a half, and she will need to be changed before you put her to bed."

"I saw Mother change your diapers when you were a baby," Eldest Brother said. "I think I remember what she did. I even helped her hang them up after they were washed."

"You won't have to do that," I said. "You'll be glad to know that the Schultzes, like most Americans, use disposable diapers. But remember: Don't try to flush them down the toilet! Put them in the can that's next to the changing table. Also, don't forget to wipe Carrie's bottom with a disposable wet towel from the box on the shelf left of the crib."

"Changing table . . . wipe bottom . . . disposable wet towel . . . left of crib . . . ," muttered Eldest Brother. His eyes began to look glassy.

Once Eldest Brother got to Carrie's room, he would find the things he needed, I thought. "Next, we'd better talk about feeding them," I continued. "You don't have to worry about Peter, since he eats grown-up food. Mrs. Schultz always has his supper on a plate all ready to eat. But Carrie eats special baby food."

"Special baby food?" asked Eldest Brother, his voice acquiring a touch of hysteria. "Does that mean I have to cook and mash things?"

"No, no," I told him quickly. "There's ready-made baby food in little glass jars, which you can find in the kitchen cupboard."

Eldest Brother nodded repeatedly, like a machine. "Glass jars . . . kitchen cupboard . . ."

"Just before bed, she has a bottle of milk, and it needs to be warmed up," I concluded briskly. I felt I had covered all the essentials. I stood up quickly and headed toward the door before Eldest Brother could change his mind about babysitting. "If you have any questions, you can call me," I added. "I'll be home all night."

I sat anxiously by the phone after Eldest Brother went off to the Schultzes'. Mother had done the same thing the first time Second Sister went out on a "non-date" with her "non-boyfriend," Paul Eng. I didn't expect anything bad to happen, but I wanted to be available. Usually Fourth Brother and I do the supper dishes together, but that night he offered to do them alone. The two of us are close, and he understood that I was worried about Eldest Brother.

When the phone rang, I grabbed it so quickly that I knocked it off the hook. I picked it up and yelled into it, "Eldest Brother! What's happened?"

There was a brief silence, and then a shaky voice said, "I represent the Society for the Preservation of Endangered Geoducks, and our truck will be in your area next Tuesday. Do you have any used clothing or furniture to donate?"

I slammed the phone down. Usually I'm more patient with telephone solicitors, but I didn't want to tie up the phone line a second longer than I had to. I went back to biting my nails.

Thirty-four minutes and seventeen seconds later, it rang again. This time I answered more cautiously. "Hello?"

"I can't find the safety pins!" cried Eldest Brother.

In the background I could hear Peter playing the violin loudly and enthusiastically. "What do you need a safety pin for?" I asked.

"I'm trying to take Carrie's diaper off," said Eldest Brother. "It's very smelly. But I don't see how to do it!"

Giggles started to bubble up my throat, but I

choked them back. "Look, you don't need to unpin the diaper. Disposable diapers are fastened by tape. You just pull them apart."

There was a pause. "Oh," Eldest Brother said, and gently hung up.

Putting the phone back on the hook, I waited for the next call for help. It came twenty-two minutes and forty seconds later. "I can't find a bottle for Carrie's milk," complained Eldest Brother. "Anyway, isn't she too old to be drinking out of a bottle?"

"She does know how to drink out of a cup," I explained, "but just before going to bed, a warm bottle comforts her and makes her sleepy. By

the way, her bottle is actually a small plastic pocket inside a carton, and Mrs. Schultz always leaves it ready for use in the refrigerator. Peter can show you where it is. All you do is heat it up."

Thirteen minutes and twelve seconds later, Eldest Brother phoned again, and I could hear the panic in his voice. "Peter decided he wanted to drink out of a bottle, too, and he finished Carrie's milk!"

Patiently, I told Eldest Brother how to insert a new plastic pocket and refill it with milk. After

I hung up, I decided that baby-sitting Eldest Brother was harder than baby-sitting Peter and Carrie!

Fourth Brother came and sat with me. "It's going to be a long night," he said.

Actually, Eldest Brother made only one more call. "Peter wants to keep on playing his violin. He refuses to go to bed!"

Peter adored the violin, and he played pretty much in tune, unlike Fourth Brother. But at least Fourth Brother was good at counting time. Peter played all the right notes; he just didn't care *when* he played them. For someone musical like Eldest Brother, it was torture to spend the evening listening to him.

I had faced this problem before, and I knew how to deal with it. "Just tell Peter," I said, "that you will make a tape of his last piece of the evening. There's a tape recorder in the living room, next to the TV set. Naturally, you have to make it clear that it's only his *last* piece that you'll tape, and promise you'll play it for his parents when they get home. He'll be tickled at having his playing captured on tape, and he'll go to bed happy."

Eldest Brother was impressed. "That's pretty clever! I'll get the cassette right away." Then he had second thoughts. "What if Peter wants to hear the tape?"

"Tell him he can listen to it tomorrow morning," I said. "By then it will be his parents' worry. But that's okay — they can't count time, either."

When Eldest Brother finally came home, he looked absolutely beat. He showed me the money he had earned, sixteen dollars.

"That's about right for one evening of babysitting," I told him.

"I need about three to four thousand dollars for a decent violin," he said slowly. "At the rate of sixteen dollars a week, I'd have to baby-sit for about . . . let's see" — he did some calculating — "more than a hundred eighty weeks. Hmmm . . . that's more than three years!"

I tried to cheer him up. "Three years will go very quickly."

"And that's just for an ordinary, passable instrument," he said in a low voice. "For something really special, like the violin I saw at Mr. Vitelli's shop, it could take centuries at this rate."

I had always admired Eldest Brother for his strength. I had seen him fearlessly climb a tall tree to rescue our cat, Rita. He could play a fiendishly hard piece of music for hours, repeating it over and over again until he got it absolutely perfect. There seemed to be nothing he couldn't do. But an evening of baby-sitting the Schultzes had drained his strength and aged him. His shoulders drooped, and he plodded upstairs like an old man. In real time it might take him three years to earn enough for a decent violin, but it would feel like fifty years.

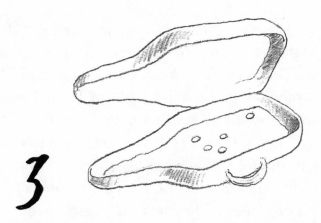

3

"I've got the perfect job for Eldest Brother!" said Fourth Brother the next day. "Mrs. Conner took me and Matthew to Pike Place Market, and we saw some musicians playing on the sidewalk. They were making good money!"

I had been to Pike Place Market before. It's popular with both Seattle people and tourists. In the covered arcade of the market, there are colorful stalls where farmers sell vegetables, fruit, and flowers. There are also shops selling fish, sausages, and other fresh meats. In addition, artists come to the market to sell pictures, sculptures, and other things they made themselves. The stalls and the cheerful chatter of the vendors reminded me of the open-air markets in China.

"I don't remember musicians at Pike Place Market," I said. "I only saw an organ grinder with a monkey. You don't expect Eldest Brother to play a hand organ, do you? Besides, where would we get a monkey?"

"I can always hop up and down, and pass a tin cup around," laughed Fourth Brother. "But seriously, Matthew and I saw a violinist and a flutist playing duets. They had their instrument cases open on the ground, and people were throwing money in."

Somehow I didn't like the idea of Eldest Brother playing in the street, with people throwing coins into his violin case. "It sounds almost like begging."

"It's not begging!" protested Fourth Brother. "He'd be earning money by playing music for people to enjoy. It's no different from playing in a concert that people buy tickets to hear."

He had a point. "And you think Eldest Brother might make real money this way?" I asked.

"The two kids we saw got a whole bunch of dollar bills, and maybe a few fives," said Fourth Brother. "And they weren't even very good. I bet Eldest Brother could make a lot more."

Maybe it was worth a try. When I mentioned playing at Pike Place Market to Eldest Brother, he reacted the way I had at first. "It's like begging!" he said, looking offended. "I need money, but not that badly!"

I used Fourth Brother's argument. "It's not begging. It's more like an outdoor concert, since you'll be performing, not passing a hat around. People who like your playing should be glad to pay."

As Eldest Brother still hesitated, I added, "Instead of changing diapers and heating bottles, you'll be doing something you love: playing the violin!"

Eldest Brother finally came around. "All right, all right, I'll give it a try. What have I got to lose, except my dignity?"

Next day, Eldest Brother and I took the bus to Pike Place Market. It was a weekday, and there weren't as many tourists as there are on weekends. We saw a man twisting a couple of long balloons into the shape of a dog, and after making barking sounds, he managed to sell the balloon dog to a little boy.

Eldest Brother frowned. "Does this mean I have to bark like a dog to attract an audience?"

I tried to put him in a good mood, and music was the thing that always worked best. "Why don't you just start playing?"

Eldest Brother opened his violin case and took out his instrument. As I had expected, once he started playing his sulkiness disappeared. He had chosen a Telemann unaccompanied sonata, a very hard piece that needed all his concentration. For him, the other people on the sidewalk became completely invisible.

I looked around. It seemed that Eldest Brother was invisible to the other people, as well. They walked past us and went about their business of buying fruit, vegetables, flowers, and embroidered aprons. True, one young girl stopped and listened for a bit and put a quarter in Eldest Brother's violin case, but then she ran off. The balloon seller was attracting more attention.

I decided to investigate the rest of the market. I had to walk almost the length of the arcade before I saw any musicians. First I heard some piping sounds. Then I saw them: two recorder players doing "Stars and Stripes Forever."

This piece is usually played by a big, brassy marching band, and hearing it played on these delicate wooden instruments was hilarious. That must have been what the players intended. A small crowd had gathered, and at the end, everyone laughed and clapped. The two teenage players, a boy and a girl, grinned broadly and made elaborate bows to the audience. The secret, it seemed, was to put on a funny act.

I put some money in a little box the players had, and I took a quick peek. There wasn't much in it, just a few coins. This didn't look like a promising way to make serious money.

I went back to Eldest Brother. He had finally attracted an audience: a couple of tourists with their arms full of flowers and Seattle souvenirs. They listened to the end of the sonata and applauded as well as they could. As the husband held the flowers, the wife opened her purse. After a struggle, she managed to fish out a dollar bill. It turned out to be the biggest piece of money Eldest Brother received that day.

But Eldest Brother looked cheerful enough. After putting away his violin, he went over to listen to the two recorder players. He burst out laughing when they launched into the opening movement of Beethoven's Fifth Symphony. Afterwards he chatted with them. I don't often see him talk with other people his age. We had always assumed he was too wrapped up in his music to care about making friends. For the first time, I began to wonder whether he was ever lonely.

When we returned from our visit to Pike Place Market, Fourth Brother asked how we did. I told him that we'd have to think of something else. "There weren't enough people there, so it would take a long time to make much money."

"Those two recorder players suggested playing at a street fair where there are mobs of people," Eldest Brother said. "They were able to make a lot more at some of those."

"Is there a street fair coming up soon?" I asked.

"Hey, there's one next weekend in Fremont!" said Fourth Brother.

On Saturday we set off for the Fremont street fair. We were lucky with the weather. In Seattle, summer is the driest season, but that doesn't mean we can always count on the sun. On the day of the street fair, however, the sky was cloudless.

Fourth Brother and I went with Eldest Brother to the fair, to give him moral support.

By the time we got to the Fremont area of town, it was getting warm, and the crowd was thick.

On both sides of the street I saw colorful booths where artists were selling their paintings, drawings, photographs, ceramics, jewelry, embroidered shirts, stuffed animals, candles. . . . Wonderful smells floated up from the food stalls: shish kebab, stir-fried noodles, garlic sausages. . . .

I was so fascinated that I almost forgot why we had come. A beautiful string of beads tempted me, and I started to reach for my wallet. The thought of money reminded me that our purpose here was to *make* money, not *spend* it. It was time for Eldest Brother to start playing and earning.

We had trouble finding a space for him to set up his music stand. Even elbow room was limited ("elbow room" is another one of my favorite American expressions). We finally found a small open area near the canal, where the crowd was thinner and a nice breeze came from the water.

"With all this noise, I don't know if anyone can hear a note," muttered Eldest Brother, as he unfolded his stand and placed his sheet music on it. The music promptly blew away.

Fourth Brother was fast, and he caught the music before it could fly into the canal. He was also prepared for the wind. He brought out two clothespins from his pocket and pinned the music back on the stand. We were ready for business.

Eldest Brother tuned his fiddle and grimaced when he heard the buzzing sound. But there was plenty of buzzing from the crowd all around us, anyway. He chose one of his favorite pieces — an unaccompanied sonata by Bach — and began to play. It was so beautiful that I closed my eyes in order to absorb the music. All the distracting noises around us seemed to retreat into the distance.

"Nobody is paying any attention," whispered Fourth Brother.

I opened my eyes and looked. He was right: The crowd pretty much ignored us. A few people glanced briefly at Eldest Brother, but most of them just went by without even turning their heads.

A little distance away, a juggler was throwing around three lit torches. His face was dead white, except for his bright-red lips and the two-inch black lashes painted around his eyes. As he juggled, he cracked jokes, but I found his dead-white face and red lips a little scary. His audience seemed to find him funny, though. Maybe Eldest Brother should try wearing make-up?

"Eldest Brother," I hissed, "I think you'll have to play something faster and louder!"

It took a few moments for Eldest Brother to cut himself off from Bach. He finally blinked and looked at me. "What was that you said?"

I pointed to the juggler and the crowd around him. "To attract people's attention, you'll have to play something a lot more showy."

He understood. In his school orchestra, the conductor knew which pieces would jar the audience awake. Looking through his music, Eldest Brother took out a fast and furious Irish jig.

"Make it nice and loud," I said to him.

Eldest Brother nodded. He threw himself into the piece, and he swayed and stomped to the music. This time he managed to stop some passersby in their tracks. Of course it helped that the juggler had stopped and gone to a booth to get himself a drink.

Eldest Brother ended the piece with a flourish of his bow in the air. Fourth Brother and I led the applause, and quite a few people joined us. A little girl toddled up unsteadily with a dollar bill that her mother had handed her. Very slowly and carefully, she placed it in Eldest Brother's violin case. Then she turned around and gave him a brilliant smile. Everybody laughed. Several other people came up and added more money.

As Eldest Brother tuned his fiddle and rubbed rosin in his bow, I took a peek at our take: several ones and a five, and some quarters. There was even a penny. Whoever threw that in was either pretty hard up, or hated Irish jigs. You can't win every time.

Now that he knew what sort of music attracted the crowd, Eldest Brother lost no time launching into a couple of other fast and furious pieces. The crowd grew, and so did the pile of money in the violin case. This was a lot better than Pike Place Market.

For a change of pace, Eldest Brother also played some lively Chinese folk tunes. When he started "The Flower Drum Song," I found an empty plastic ice-cream bucket, turned it upside down, and pounded on it like a drum as accompaniment. The audience liked that, and more money poured in.

We had to take a break after two more pieces. The day was getting pretty hot, and Fourth

Brother offered to get us some drinks. He didn't come back for a long time, so Eldest Brother decided to start playing again. But strangely enough, he could no longer attract a good crowd. Even a dazzling capriccio by Paganini drew only four listeners.

Fourth Brother came back finally with three lemonades. "Where were you?" I asked him. "We're dying of thirst!"

"I was listening to our competition," he said. "Do you hear that?"

The sound of a violin floated toward us along the canal. I listened to a few measures of Mozart. It wasn't the most exciting performance I'd ever heard, but at least all the notes were there. "That doesn't sound like much competition," I said.

"She's got a big crowd, though," said Fourth Brother. "I think you'd better take a look."

I followed him toward the sound of the music. As we got closer, the crowd got thicker. Then I saw the performer and knew why we couldn't compete. The violinist was a little girl around four years old. She had a huge mop of golden curls and wore a pink dress trimmed all over with lace.

"We've got problems," I muttered. Eldest

Brother didn't stand a chance against a competitor like that.

"You know, she's not too bad," said Eldest Brother, who had come up with his fiddle in his hands. "I rather like her phrasing."

I listened more closely, and decided he was right. The girl was too timid to put much expression into her playing, but she seemed to know what Mozart was about.

She did have trouble with one passage, though. She couldn't seem to manage the ornament — the little twiddly bit. Suddenly I heard the phrase played behind me. Eldest Brother couldn't resist showing the girl how the passage should sound.

The girl whipped around and stared. Then she picked up her bow and played the passage again. "Like this?" she asked.

"Not quite," said Eldest Brother. He played the same phrase, more slowly.

The girl nodded and tried again, and this time she got it right. She continued with the piece, and Eldest Brother joined her by playing an upper part that he made up on the spot. The girl's father, who was standing nearby, frowned at us. Apparently he felt that Eldest Brother was trying to force himself into the act.

But the crowd liked the duet. At the end of the piece, there was clapping and even some whistling. Money poured into the girl's little violin case. Her father beamed and came up to us. "Hey, Lisa's got herself a free violin lesson here."

"She's not bad," Eldest Brother said, and smiled at the girl.

The father looked thoughtfully at the heap of money in his daughter's violin case. His eyes narrowed as he calculated. "Say, maybe the two of you could do a joint act. We could split the take fifty-fifty, and we'd still wind up ahead."

Eldest Brother looked startled. "Well . . ."

"Why don't you join her?" I said to him.

"Yeah, that's a good idea," said Fourth Brother.

So Eldest Brother joined the little girl in pink, and they played several more duets. He stopped a few times to point out how she could improve some passage or another. The crowd seemed to like that.

The father was delighted with their success. "It must be the novelty. People never saw a public music lesson before."

Personally, I'd pay money to *avoid* having to listen to a music lesson. But I saw his point.

Lisa, the little girl, was genuinely musical, and it was very satisfying to hear her getting even better.

"You know, I've taken Lisa to several street fairs," continued the father, "but this is the most we've ever made."

Eldest Brother wasn't doing badly either, I thought. What with the money he had made earlier . . .

Then I yelped as I suddenly realized that Eldest Brother had brought only his violin with him. "What did you do with all the money in your own violin case?"

Eldest Brother's jaw dropped. "I . . . I . . . I guess it's still in the same place."

We raced back to the spot near the canal where he had left his stuff. His violin case was still on the ground, and inside were the quarters and other coins. But all the paper money was gone!

The three of us just stood there, too crushed to speak. I had to bite down hard on my lips to keep myself from crying.

There was a sound of running steps. The white-faced juggler rushed up holding some bills in his hand. His bright-red lips cracked open in a smile. "These are yours, I believe.

They were blowing away and I managed to rescue some of them."

I was surprised and touched. Eldest Brother managed to stammer out his thanks, but the juggler just shook his head. "No problem. I know what it's like to work hard. You had a class act there, and you don't deserve to lose all your earnings."

With the money the little girl's father gave Eldest Brother and what the juggler had rescued, we had about thirty dollars. It was a better than baby-sitting, at least. But it still didn't go far to pay for a violin.

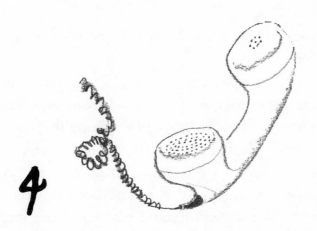

4

I love listening to Father and Eldest Brother when the two of them practice a duet together. It's inspiring to see them so totally wrapped up in the music. Father is always beaming when they finish practicing, and I can tell how happy he is believing that his son can become a great violinist someday. The rest of us aren't even jealous of Eldest Brother. We've all accepted the fact that he's the best musician in the family, and we're proud that he's our brother.

But this evening there was no smile on Father's face when they finished playing. Something was not going well. Eldest Brother put down his violin and sighed. "I'm sorry," he said. "I can't seem to concentrate. The buzzing didn't bother me when I played at the street fair, but with serious music I can tell that it's getting really bad."

Father frowned. "We'll have to think about renting a violin for you. I'm afraid it's out of the question for us to buy a new one right now."

Even coming up with the money to rent a violin would be a problem. But at least it wasn't hopeless, especially if Eldest Brother went on with his baby-sitting and playing in the street.

I went with Eldest Brother when he set out for Mr. Vitelli's shop, since my cello bow needed a bit of work. Fortunately, it was a simple job to fix the bow, and Mr. Vitelli's son, Andreas, did it for me free of charge. He was a nice young man who towered over his father. While Mr. Vitelli was small and dark, Andreas was very tall, with reddish blond hair. But his fingers had the same delicate touch as his father's.

While I was having my bow fixed, Eldest Brother and Mr. Vitelli were talking earnestly at the other end of the shop. I saw them shaking their heads sadly.

"So how much does it cost to rent a violin?" I asked Eldest Brother as we got ready to leave.

"All the good ones are expensive," he said glumly. "I'd have to use up most of the money I've made so far."

"Can't you put up with a cheaper instrument?" I asked. Then I added quickly, "Until you earn enough for a good fiddle, that is."

"In that case, I might as well stick to my buzzing violin," he muttered.

As we walked to the door, Eldest Brother paused and looked wistfully back at the shelf of instruments. I saw what he was staring at: the shining, beautiful violin that he had fallen in love with.

I felt very sorry for him. Eldest Brother would have to play at hundreds of street fairs before he could make enough money to buy it. Meanwhile, it must be torture to look at the instrument and know that somebody else might buy it any day.

Mrs. O'Meara, Kim's mother, invited me to dinner that evening. She said Kim was eating at my house so often that she was doing better with chopsticks than with a knife and fork, and it was time to even the score a little. I protested that my mother didn't mind having guests for dinner. I wasn't just being polite, since all Mother had to do was set another pair of chopsticks and fill another bowl of rice.

But I was glad to accept Mrs. O'Meara's invitation. I wanted every chance I could get to experience eating a normal American meal with a normal American family.

Kim had told her family about Eldest Brother's attempts to earn money. "Is your brother having any luck?" asked Mr. O'Meara. "I remember how tough it was when I was that age. I dreamed day and night about earning enough to buy a motorcycle, and I tried my hand at just about everything."

I looked at Mr. O'Meara in his suit and his tie and his well-polished shoes. He had just the beginning of a potbelly, and his hair was starting to grow thin at the top of his head. It was awfully hard to picture him on a motorcycle.

He must have noticed my expression. "It was from seeing the movie *Easy Rider*," he explained. "While *my* father dreamed about roaming the Wild West as a cowboy on a white horse, my friends and I dreamed about roaming the country on a motorcycle."

Kim looked impressed. "Wow, Dad, you never told us about your motorcycle!"

Mr. O'Meara grinned ruefully. "That's because I never made enough money from summer jobs to buy one." Then he cleared his throat and turned back to me. "So how did your brother do? Did he manage to earn anything?"

I told the O'Mearas about the baby-sitting and the street fair. "We made almost thirty dollars in one day at the Fremont fair. It would have been more if the wind hadn't blown away half our money. Too bad there isn't a fair every week."

"Your brother could play at the waterfront, and other places where there are lots of tourists," suggested Mrs. O'Meara.

I told the O'Mearas about our experiences at Pike Place Market. "Since the crowd wasn't as thick as at a street fair, the performers weren't making much."

"Don't worry, the money will add up bit by bit," Mr. O'Meara said. "By the way, does your brother have a savings account?"

My mouth fell open. Opening a bank account made Eldest Brother's earnings sound like big time. A bank account was something adults had, a place where Father put what was left of his salary. I was just clicking my mouth shut when Mr. O'Meara added, "And he should really get some CDs."

Get CDs? I just couldn't figure out how buying music might help Eldest Brother. But since Mr. O'Meara worked for an insurance company and understood financial mysteries, I resolved to pass his advice on to Eldest Brother.

Before I could ask him to explain, the phone rang. Mrs. O'Meara went over to answer, and I heard her say, "No thanks, we don't need any."

She came back to the table frowning. "Someone selling a new kind of polyester shingle they claim will last five hundred years!"

Kim snorted. "Our house will be all rotten by then, we'll all be gone, and the only thing left will be the shingles!"

"Say," said Mr. O'Meara, snapping his fingers. "Maybe your brother can do telemarketing." He explained that telemarketing consists of calling up people and asking them whether they want to buy some merchandise or subscribe to some magazine or service. "I bet there are lots of telemarketing agencies to check, considering how many calls we get."

I remembered all the calls we get about donations to some society or another. Somebody must be making them, so why not Eldest Brother? Dialing a phone is a lot less strenuous than baby-sitting or playing violin in the street.

"Why don't I see what I can find?" offered Mr. O'Meara.

He kept his promise, and two days later he told us about a telemarketing job opening at a company called Ah, Wilderness!, which made outdoor equipment entirely from natural fibers. Their tents, hiking boots, socks, shirts, and parkas used only leather, wool, cotton, silk, cashmere, and linen — not a single nylon, orlon, acrylic, or polyester fiber went into any of the gear. To compile a mailing list for their catalog, they wanted telemarketers to call up potential customers.

Eldest Brother wasn't too keen on the job. Of the four of us, he's the one with the strongest Chinese accent, and he's sensitive about it. With his fine musician's ear, he gets the intonation right — that is, his melody is perfect. But he has trouble with some of the English consonants, especially *b* and *d*.

I speak English the best, since I work hardest at it. Fourth Brother is pretty good, too. I think being young helps. Second Sister has a good accent, even if she claims that English is an unnatural language and she will never feel at home in it.

"People would have a hard time even understanding me on the phone," Eldest Brother said. "And besides, Mr. O'Meara says I'd have to do the calling from midafternoon till nine, because that's the best time for catching people at home."

I saw the problem. It would mean that Eldest Brother would have to work during dinnertime.

Meals are very important to Chinese families. My mother told me that when she was young, you always greeted a friend by asking, "Have you eaten?" instead of "How are you?" The friend was supposed to say, "Yes, I've eaten," because if they confessed they hadn't eaten, you would be forced to invite them to dinner.

"Why do you talk so much about dinner?" Kim once asked me. "And also about lunch and breakfast?"

I tried to think of an answer. "Maybe it's because there are so many people in China, and having enough food to go around has always been a problem. Plus, eating together makes us feel like a family, and family means everything to us."

I couldn't blame Eldest Brother for not wanting to take the telemarketing job. He would not be able to eat dinner with the rest of us, and he would interrupt other people at *their* dinner, which we consider very rude.

But I couldn't help noticing that he had been practicing less lately. Father was quick to notice, too. "Yingwu, you really need a new instrument," he said heavily. "Maybe I can go to the bank and try to borrow some money."

Although our family wasn't rich, we'd never borrowed money before. We don't own a car or a house, and for everything else we pay cash on the spot. Many Chinese people feel it's shameful to borrow money.

"No, no, don't do that!" Eldest Brother said quickly. He sighed. "I'll try the telemarketing job Mr. O'Meara was talking about."

The first time Eldest Brother went off to do his job, I was as nervous as the time when he went to baby-sit the Schultzes. As soon as he came home that night, I rushed over to him. "So how was it?" I demanded.

Mother was at the door, too. "Come into the kitchen, Yingwu," she said to Eldest Brother. "You'd better have a bite to eat. You must be starving."

Eldest Brother walked slowly into the kitchen, sat down on a chair, and picked up the bowl of rice that Mother had left for him. It wasn't until he had swallowed a couple of mouthfuls that he finally broke his silence. "It's not that the work is really hard. . . ."

I waited impatiently, but he picked up some pickled cucumbers and munched on them, before eating another mouthful of rice. At first he looked too tired to have much appetite, but he got hungrier as he ate, and he polished off a plate full of stir-fried pork and green peppers, as well as two bowls of rice. I poured him some orange juice.

Finally he was ready to talk. "There were fourteen of us, and we sat in a room full of telephones. Our boss gave us each some pages from a phone book, and we had to call all the numbers and ask a list of questions. If we got a positive answer on more than half the questions, we'd offer to send the person a catalog."

"What sort of questions?" I asked. I was curious about the kind of thing Ah, Wilderness! wanted to know.

Eldest Brother didn't answer right away. He drank some more juice and brooded. Suddenly he cried, "I felt so foolish!"

"Why? What was on your list of questions?" I asked, surprised.

"I had to ask people whether they hiked or climbed mountains, and how often they went camping," he said in a low voice.

"What's wrong with asking them that?" asked Fourth Brother. He had joined us in the kitchen and was pouring himself a glass of juice.

"The second person I called told me she was an eighty-four-year-old woman crippled by arthritis," said Eldest Brother. "But I still had to go through with the list of questions my boss handed me. So I had to ask her whether she camped or hiked or climbed mountains, and whether she wore woolen or nylon parkas."

I pictured the eighty-four-year-old woman, forced to stay home because of arthritis, having to tell some young kid on the phone whether she climbed mountains. "Did she get mad at you?"

"No, she was very patient," muttered Eldest Brother. "She even laughed a little. But I felt so stupid asking her those questions!"

"But not everyone you called was an old lady," I said to Eldest Brother.

"I got a couple of working mothers who told me that they had just got home and had to prepare dinner for their families, and didn't have time to worry about felt tents," said Eldest Brother.

"Didn't you get anybody who liked the wilderness and camping, hiking, and climbing mountains?" asked Fourth Brother.

"Yes, I got a few," admitted Eldest Brother. "One girl said she would love to have a parka made of real silk. Only she turned out to be nine years old, and she hung up on me when I told her the price of a silk parka started at three hundred and fifty dollars. Many of the people who answered the phone told me they didn't give a . . . um . . . about tents made of felt."

I knew he skipped a naughty word he thought Fourth Brother and I were too young to hear. In fact, I suspected that he must have heard a great many naughty words while working that evening.

"One man shouted at me and said that silk parkas didn't last," continued Eldest Brother. "He said polyester ones can last as long as five hundred years!"

I burst out laughing and told Eldest Brother about the telemarketer who had called the O'Mearas. "He tried to sell them polyester shingles that would last five hundred years! I bet it's the same guy!"

After a moment Eldest Brother's lips twitched, and even he broke out laughing.

"So how much money did you make?" I finally asked. That was the whole point of the job, after all.

"I got paid minimum wage," said Eldest Brother. "I made a little over forty dollars."

"That's a lot better than baby-sitting, and it's lighter work!" I said, trying to cheer him up. He admitted that it was easier work and provided a more reliable income than playing in the street.

"It's also more dignified than putting your violin case on the ground to catch coins," I added.

"I'm not sure it *is* more dignified," muttered Eldest Brother.

I knew what he meant. It must have been terribly embarrassing to interrupt people in the middle of dinner and ask them about tents.

"At least the money is good in telemarketing," said Eldest Brother. A dreamy look appeared on his face, and I suspected he was thinking about Mr. Vitelli's violin.

"At least the money is good . . ." That phrase would haunt me in the days that followed.

5

"I was talking with Paul," Second Sister said a few days later.

"You mean your non-boyfriend?" I couldn't resist teasing her. Second Sister's face reddened, but she ignored the question and continued. "He was saying that he made a lot of money last summer being a busboy. I bet Eldest Brother can do it, too."

The rest of us stared at her. Eldest Brother was the one who broke the silence. "But I can't drive!"

Second Sister laughed. "No, silly, being a busboy doesn't mean you drive a bus! It means you carry away dirty dishes in a restaurant!"

I took out my notebook and hurriedly added an entry, *busboy*. It wasn't often that I learned an English phrase from Second Sister.

Mother looked doubtful. "It's not easy being a waiter. The customers get mad at you if you get an order wrong, and it's an extremely tiring job."

"Being a waiter and being a busboy are different," explained Second Sister. "Paul explained it all to me. Busboys don't need as much experience because they just clear the tables and they don't have to take orders. Of course, they also get less money. In most restaurants, the waiters give a portion of their tips to the busboys."

Our family aren't exactly experts on tipping, because in China you don't tip people. You pay what's on the check, and that's it. When we first came to America, my parents got a lot of dirty looks from waiters. Finally one of them demanded to know what it was they didn't like about the service. The waiter thought my parents didn't leave a tip because it was their way of telling him the service was lousy.

The whole thing was so embarrassing that my parents left an enormous tip at the next restaurant they went to. They couldn't understand why the waiter gasped with delight. Finally my parents learned that the normal tip was around 15 percent of the bill. That made waiting in a restaurant sound like a pretty good job to me.

"If you're willing to do that kind of work, Paul can speak to his old boss about getting a job for you," continued Second Sister.

"What about Paul himself?" I asked. "Doesn't he have a summer job, too?"

"He's flipping hamburgers at a fast-food restaurant," said Fourth Brother. "It's pretty hard work, especially during the lunch hour, but it pays well." Fourth Brother was always up to date on what Paul was doing, because he was getting baseball coaching from him. He added, "Paul says he wants to keep his evenings free."

I suddenly realized that Second Sister had been doing less baby-sitting recently. She apparently wanted to keep her evenings free, too.

Paul was busy, but not too busy to take Eldest Brother to the Mandarin Duck restaurant, and Eldest Brother started work that very night. He returned home tired, but not as depressed as he was after an evening of telemarketing.

"What sort of food do they serve at the Mandarin Duck?" asked Mother.

"They call it mandarin food," Eldest Brother said, shaking his head. "But when I asked people what mandarin food is, nobody really knew."

We were puzzled when we came to America

and heard the word "mandarin" for the first time. It isn't a Chinese word, and in America it can mean all sorts of things. By a "mandarin" Americans sometimes mean an official in the old days, what we call a *guan*. At other times Americans use the word to mean *putong hua*, a dialect spoken by the majority of the Chinese, and now the official national language. And then there's a duck called a mandarin duck. Grocery stores even label tangerines as mandarin oranges sometimes. It's all very confusing!

Eldest Brother was happy with his night's work. He came home with almost fifty dollars. The waiters gave one-tenth of their tips to the busboy who cleared their tables, and since Eldest Brother cleared for several waiters, his share was pretty good.

"Wow!" I said. "How much do you have now?"

Eldest Brother took out his savings-account passbook. It showed what he had earned from an evening of baby-sitting, the take from the street fair, and the pay from three nights of telemarketing. If he added the fifty dollars from busing dishes, he would have more than two hundred dollars!

It sounded like a fabulous sum. Mr. Vitelli's

violin probably cost several thousand dollars, but Eldest Brother had made a good start, at least.

Then I remembered something Kim's father had said. "Mr. O'Meara advises you to buy CDs," I told him. "That's supposed to make your money grow faster."

Eldest Brother didn't believe me. "How can that possibly make my money grow faster?"

"I don't know," I admitted. "But Mr. O'Meara knows a lot about money, so it's a good idea to do what he says. Just think! This is your chance to buy the Menuhin-Kempff recordings of the Beethoven violin sonatas you always wanted!"

"Are you sure Mr. O'Mears meant CD records?" asked Eldest Brother, still not quite convinced. "You'd better check to make sure."

I was surprised. I knew how much he had yearned for those Beethoven CDs. Now he not only had the money, but also the perfect excuse to buy the records. In his place I would have rushed down to the record store immediately.

But Eldest Brother just climbed slowly upstairs. In the old days he would have bounced up to his room and put in several hours of hard practice. Of course, he had a right to be exhausted after busing dishes all evening, I reminded myself.

Next day I decided to check with Kim about the CDs. It *was* hard to imagine how buying records could make money grow, even recordings of a great composer like Beethoven. Kim was also baffled, but promised to ask her father to explain.

The phone rang as we were eating dinner that night. I wondered if it was someone saving geoducks, selling felt tents, or installing polyester shingles that lasted five hundred years. Second Sister rushed to answer the phone. These days she was usually the one who got to the phone first. She came back more slowly and told me it was Kim.

"What Dad meant by a CD was a *certificate of deposit!*" Kim told me. "It's something for investing your money, and it has a higher interest rate than a savings account. He didn't mean a *compact disc!*"

When Eldest Brother returned from the Mandarin Duck and heard what Kim had told me, he smiled with relief. "Good thing I didn't buy those Beethoven CDs after all. Think of all the money I would have wasted!"

Again he surprised me. He had called buying

the Beethoven records a waste of money! Imagine saying that about Beethoven!

That made me realize that I hadn't heard Eldest Brother play the violin for three whole days. I didn't remember his ever going for more than twenty-four hours without playing his violin. On the very day we arrived in America, after a flight of fourteen hours from China, he took out his violin and played the first movement of Beethoven's Spring Sonata to celebrate. That was before we even unpacked our luggage. Why was he neglecting his violin now? Did the buzzing bother him that much?

We ran into Mr. O'Meara a couple of days later, and we all laughed about the mix-up over the CDs. Mr. O'Meara said that he had been eating at a Japanese restaurant and discovered they needed another waiter. Would Eldest Brother like to apply for the job? It paid a lot better than busing.

"But I'm not Japanese!" protested Eldest Brother.

"Oh, that's okay," Mr. O'Meara said comfortably. "The customers won't be able to tell the difference."

I was a bit offended when I heard him say that. Before we moved to Seattle, I had seen very few Japanese people. In Chinese schools we were taught that they were our enemies because Japan had invaded our country during the Second World War. All Japanese people were bowlegged and had buckteeth, we were told. Of course, many Americans thought all *Chinese* people were bowlegged and had buckteeth. They couldn't tell us apart from the Japanese.

To my surprise, Eldest Brother wasn't bothered by the idea of working in a Japanese restaurant. He smiled and said that his social studies teacher was Mrs. Nomura, and she was Japanese-American. She was very helpful and patient with him when he first arrived. From the way he smiled, I gathered that she did not have bowlegs or buckteeth.

"But I don't have any experience waiting on tables," Eldest Brother pointed out. "It's a lot harder than busing dishes."

"Well, they're so anxious to get waiters that they're willing to take you on and give you training on the job," said Mr. O'Meara.

That made me suspicious. "Why are they so desperate? And why can't they use Japanese teenagers if they need waiters so much?"

"Because there aren't that many Japanese

teenagers around," explained Mr. O'Meara. "The ones who come to Seattle are students or tourists, and they usually bring enough money with them."

Eldest Brother needed the money. So he quit his busing job at the Mandarin Duck and went to work at the Sushi Hi, which was the name of the Japanese restaurant. Mr. O'Meara had to explain the name to us. Apparently sushi is a kind of Japanese dish that's getting very popular in America. It typically involves raw fish. I gag at the thought of eating raw fish, but since many Americans also eat rare roast beef (yuck!), raw fish shouldn't bother them. At least it doesn't leave a pool of blood on your plate.

"Why the word 'hi' in the name?" I asked. "Is it some kind of greeting?"

"No, it's a play on words," explained Mr. O'Meara. "You see, the Japanese word for 'yes' is pronounced just like 'hi.' So when you say the name of the restaurant, it sounds like, 'Yes, I want some sushi.'"

Eldest Brother went off to work cheerfully enough, and if he was bothered by the thought of serving raw fish, he didn't show it. He came back looking even more cheerful and told us gleefully that he had made nearly seventy dollars. On a weekend night, he might make even more.

We were all curious to find out what Japanese food was like. "They use a lot of soy sauce, don't they?" asked Mother. "And they eat rice with chopsticks. So it can't be too different from Chinese food."

Eldest Brother shook his head. "Japanese food is *very* different. I tried a few things, and it's like nothing I've had before. We waiters are allowed to eat anything on the menu, except for a few of the very expensive items."

"Did you find anything you liked?" I asked.

"There's a dish called tempura," replied Eldest Brother. "It consists of prawns, fish, and various vegetables covered with batter and deep-fried. It was delicious!"

"What were the expensive items you didn't get to eat?" asked Fourth Brother.

"Some of the raw seafood," said Eldest Brother. "One was something called sea urchin's eggs. Frankly, I was perfectly happy to do without it."

"I'm getting really curious about Japanese food," I said to Kim the next day. "Sushi seems to be very popular, and also something called teriyaki. In fact, I see lots of teriyaki cafes in town. I'm tempted to try some."

"Hey, maybe I can get my dad to take us to the Sushi Hi," said Kim. "It's one of his favorite restaurants."

Mr. O'Meara was glad to oblige. Anyway, he wanted to see how Eldest Brother was doing, since he was responsible for finding him the job.

A couple of nights later, Kim and I found ourselves seated at the Sushi Hi with Mr. and Mrs. O'Meara. My whole family was invited, but the others wanted to wait and hear my report on Japanese food before they took a chance on it.

Eldest Brother saw us come in, but after greeting us briefly he didn't come near us, since he was waiting on tables at the other side of the restaurant. I think we embarrassed him a little, because it looked like we were checking up on him.

I tried to read the menu. None of it made any sense to me, so I had to ask Mr. O'Meara to explain.

"Personally, I always start with a few pieces of sushi," he explained.

A big plate of sushi arrived, consisting of small lumps of rice covered with various toppings. Since the name of the restaurant was

Sushi Hi, I figured this must be their specialty, so I decided to try a piece. Some of the toppings were obviously raw fish, and I avoided those. I finally settled on a piece wrapped in a wrinkly brown skin that looked like fried tofu. We eat a lot of tofu, so I thought this was a safe choice.

When I bit into the piece of sushi and started to chew, several sensations hit me at the same time. First of all, the rice was cold! In China, beggars are the only ones who have to eat cold, leftover rice. Also, the rice in the sushi was sticky. But what I found strangest was the taste: Not only was it both salty and sweet, it was also sour! Sour rice usually means it's spoiled. I chewed and chewed on the gummy mouthful of salty-sweet-sour rice, but I couldn't bring myself to swallow it.

Mrs. O'Meara saw my expression. "You don't have to eat it if you don't like it," she said kindly. "I had a hard time getting used to sushi, myself."

I quietly spat my mouthful of rice into a paper napkin and turned to see what Kim was eating. She had a plate of cut-up broiled chicken in a brown sauce. "This is teriyaki," she explained. "Want some?"

I tried a piece and found it not too bad. It was

a bit too sweet for my taste, but otherwise it was pretty good. At least it was warm.

Mr. O'Meara was dipping a piece of sushi in a mixture made from a green paste and some soy sauce. That might improve the flavor of the sushi, I thought. Following his example, I smeared a dollop of green paste on another piece of sushi and quickly popped it in my mouth.

"Careful, that's hot!" warned Kim. But she was already too late.

At first I didn't find the taste so hot. I had eaten Hunan food that was twice as hot as this. The next instant, though, I felt something drilling through the roof of my mouth, all the way through my brains, and exploding out the top of my head. For several minutes all I could do was make *hoo-hoo* sounds.

"Here, you'd better take a mouthful of plain rice," offered Mrs. O'Meara.

I snatched the rice and stuffed some into my mouth. Eventually my eyes stopped watering and I could talk again. "Wow!" I croaked. "Too bad I didn't have this around for the Fourth of July fireworks!"

"That green stuff is called wasabi," said Mr. O'Meara. "I've learned to treat it with respect."

I took out my notebook and entered *wasabi*. Most of my entries are in English, but I thought this green dynamite could be a useful weapon to keep in reserve.

The waiter brought us a plate of deep-fried prawns, yams, fish, and green peppers. This time I was more cautious and tried it without using any sauce. It was delicious.

"This dish is called tempura," said Mr. O'Meara. "Apparently the Japanese learned it from the Portuguese back in the sixteenth century."

So this was what Eldest Brother liked best, too. I looked around and spotted him talking and laughing with some customers at the far end of the room. Later, I saw him talking to one of the waitresses. He was smiling and seemed relaxed and happy.

When we got ready to leave, I thanked the O'Mearas politely for treating me to my first Japanese meal. Mr. O'Meara looked at me. "I don't think it was all that much of a treat, was it, Mary?"

"The teriyaki was pretty good and the tempura was delicious!" I was able to say truthfully.

"But the sushi was a bit of a shock for you," said Mrs. O'Meara.

"I'm surprised!" said Kim. "I thought Chinese food and Japanese food were similar. You both use chopsticks and everything."

"Not even the chopsticks are alike," I told her. "Chinese chopsticks have blunt ends, and Japanese chopsticks have sharp, pointy ends."

"The better to stab your sushi with, in case the raw fish is still moving?" asked Kim.

When I got home, my family wanted to know what the food was like. "I liked the teriyaki and the tempura," I said. "But I didn't like the cold, gummy rice in the sushi. And you have to be careful of anything covered with a pale green paste."

"How is Eldest Brother doing?" Mother asked anxiously. "Is he finding the work too hard?"

"He's doing fine," I told her. "In fact, he looks quite happy at the Sushi Hi."

I suddenly realized that Eldest Brother actually looked like a normal teenage boy as he chatted with the other waiters. He had always been a loner interested only in music, but at the restaurant he was enjoying the company of other young people. In spite of the hard work, he didn't come home depressed, with shoulders drooping from exhaustion, as he had with some of his other jobs.

That night, I watched Eldest Brother going briskly upstairs, whistling a passage from Beethoven's Archduke Trio. That is one of my favorite pieces, and it's so beautiful that it practically melts my bones. I used to play the cello part in the trio, while Mother played the piano and Eldest Brother, the violin. We hadn't touched the piece in months, though. Just hearing the notes again brought a lump into my throat.

What made me sad was that Eldest Brother only *whistled* the passage; he didn't play it on his violin.

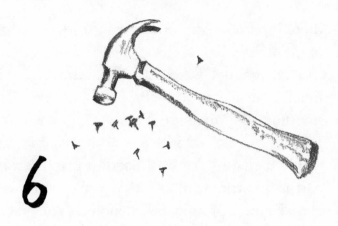

6

"I bet you've got enough money to spare to rent a violin now," I said to Eldest Brother. "Then you can go back to practicing."

He shook his head. "The practicing can wait."

That shocked me. I remembered the times when he came home in the rain, and without even bothering to change out of his wet clothes, he would take out his violin to practice some passage he was worried about.

He was different in another way, too. After coming home from the restaurant, he would immediately take out the brown envelope where he kept his cash and add up the night's earnings. With shining eyes, he would calculate the total. He went to the bank every Monday morning the minute it opened and deposited his weekly earnings into his savings account. Eldest Brother, who had never cared about money before, wasn't acting like himself.

"But you've got lots of money saved up!" I said to him. "You should rent a decent violin now."

"I don't want to use any of my savings to *rent* an instrument," he said, shaking his head.

I finally understood. He was desperately saving up money to buy Mr. Vitelli's violin, the one he had set his heart on. But could he really earn money fast enough?

It also bothered me that our quartet didn't play together anymore. With some pushing from Eldest Brother, we used to play together every week, even if it was just for an hour. I missed the quartet. I had my very own part in a quartet, so it was more fun than playing in an orchestra with lots of other cellists playing the same part.

Second Sister, Matthew, and I tried to play trios together, but without Eldest Brother a spark was missing somehow. It'd been a long time since we heard him say, "Come on, everybody! Let's try that rondo again!"

I mentioned my worries to Fourth Brother, who was in the kitchen busily stuffing bean sprouts between two slices of bread. He was taking the sandwich with him to the playfield, where he was going to play in an informal baseball game between our neighborhood team and the one from the Madrona neighborhood. There was just a mouthful left in the dish of bean sprouts, so Fourth Brother stuffed the rest into his mouth. With his terrible ear, he never understood Eldest Brother's dedication to music, but the two of us were close and he tried to cheer me up. "How about coming to our game?" he asked, wrapping up his sandwich. "It'll take your mind off your worries."

I needed more than a baseball game to distract me. As I hesitated, he added, "Second Sister is coming to the game."

That surprised me. I didn't think Second Sister had the slightest interest in baseball. Soccer was her game.

Fourth Brother had a sly grin. "Paul, her 'non-boyfriend,' is the coach of our team, you know."

I had to laugh, and I felt my spirits lift. I decided to go to the game, after all.

I found an empty seat near Second Sister, who was there early. She raised her eyebrows when she saw me. "What are *you* doing here? I didn't know you were all that keen on base-ball."

"I was just about to ask you the same thing," I said innocently. "I thought you only liked soc-cer."

Second Sister blushed and looked away. "It was time to widen my interests."

We settled down to watch the game, and I was surprised to find that Second Sister knew quite a bit about baseball. She must have re-ceived some coaching from the coach.

Our team won easily. Fourth Brother hit a double, and Second Sister and I were both de-lighted. His ambition was to hit a home run. He hadn't done it yet, but he hadn't lost hope. With Paul's coaching, he might even do it some day.

While Fourth Brother and Second Sister were talking to Paul after the game, I found myself next to Mr. and Mrs. Conner. Matthew was also on the team, and he had driven in two runs.

"Say, what's this I hear about your brother having trouble with his fiddle?" asked Mr. Con-ner.

Matthew had real musical talent, but it had taken us a while to convince his parents that he had a future as a violinist. Mr. Conner was now openly proud of his son's playing. Sometimes

Matthew was even a little embarrassed when his father boasted about him at school concerts and PTA meetings.

I told Mr. and Mrs. Conner about how expensive it was to fix the violin, and how hard Eldest Brother was working to earn money for a new one.

"Great!" said Mr. Conner. "I admire a kid who doesn't wait for handouts from other people and earns the money on his own!"

Was this what most Americans believed? It was certainly different from what the Chinese people believed, that the government should help talented people like Eldest Brother.

"But isn't a violin terribly expensive?" asked Mrs. Conner. "Matthew is renting one. We went to Mr. Vitelli's shop to look around, but when we found out how much the instruments cost, we decided to rent instead."

"I just about keeled over when I saw the price on one little fiddle," said Mr. Conner. "Well, I wish your brother luck."

"He's putting money away in his savings account," I said. "He can make more than seventy dollars a night working in a restaurant."

"Tell him to keep up the good work!" said

Mr. Conner. He was about to leave, but turned back. He must have noticed my expression. "What's the matter, kid? The money coming in too slowly?"

I nodded. "He's got his heart set on a really beautiful violin in Mr. Vitelli's shop, but I'm afraid it's going to be very expensive. It might take many years for him to earn enough to buy it."

"What's wrong?" asked Matthew, coming up to join his parents.

"Mary here says her brother wants to buy an expensive violin," said Mrs. Conner. "But it might take him a long time to earn enough money for it."

Mr. Conner was looking very thoughtful. "I think I may be able to help, but I need to talk to my boss. I'll call you tomorrow."

Mr. Conner is a carpenter, and he was working on a construction job at a housing development. Carpentry was the one interest Eldest Brother had besides music, and he and Mr. Conner often discussed this hammer or that, or which nail to use.

Mr. Conner kept his promise. The very next day, he came over to our house and said he could give Eldest Brother some construction work.

Eldest Brother's eyes lit up. "How much does it pay?"

"A hundred dollars a day, if you work hard," replied Mr. Conner.

"Wow!" said Eldest Brother. "That's even better than waiting tables! I'd like to give it a try. That is, if you think I can do it."

"I've seen you at work before," said Mr. Conner, "so I've got confidence in you."

Eldest Brother began to look unsure. "Yes, but the construction work must be more complicated than just repairing our front steps. I don't want to do something wrong and cause trouble between you and your boss."

"I won't give you anything to do that I'm not sure about," said Mr. Conner. "We'll start with a few jobs you can manage without any problem. They aren't complicated — boring, maybe, but not complicated."

So Eldest Brother added construction work to his list of jobs. Matthew took Fourth Brother and me to the construction site, and we watched from across the street. Inside a cyclone fence, about a dozen wooden houses were being built on a huge lot overlooking the freeway. The houses were pretty much all alike, but they would be painted different colors when they were finished, Matthew said.

I couldn't help thinking how different this was from China. In a big Chinese city, almost everyone lives in an apartment house. A few of the old houses were one-story buildings arranged around a courtyard, but all the new houses were tall apartments. I couldn't remember seeing a single *new* house in China like these wooden ones, built for just one family alone. I finally understood why Mother keeps saying, "There is so much space in America!"

We could see Eldest Brother inside the cyclone fence, putting nails into the wooden frame of a house. I didn't recognize him at first, since he was wearing a metal helmet. I only picked him out because he was more lightly built than the other workmen. As I watched him swinging his hammer and moving easily around, I was proud of him. Then I wondered to myself, What if he does this for the rest of his life? It was a good job, and he seemed to like it. But it would mean giving up a musical career. The thought brought a lump to my throat.

Matthew seemed to feel the same way. "Let's go," he said quietly. "We don't want to bother the workers."

So Eldest Brother worked on the construction site from eight to four every day. He came home and washed up, and then was off to the Sushi Hi every evening. He was always utterly exhausted when he came home at night. Still, he was never too tired to count up all his earnings.

I started to be afraid that after a full day's work on the construction site, Eldest Brother would arrive at the Sushi Hi already tired. He might drop a tray of food, or spill a drink on a customer. I'd even heard of a customer suing because somebody had spilled a hot drink on him.

I began dropping by the construction site regularly to see how hard Eldest Brother was working and whether he could stand the pace. Fourth Brother was too busy to worry much about Eldest Brother. He was totally involved with baseball and getting coaching from Paul. And Second Sister was getting involved with baseball, as well.

On my third visit to the site, some of the other workers recognized me and called out a greeting. Eldest Brother didn't look in my direction. Maybe he was embarrassed, like the time when we went to check on him at the Sushi Hi. Or maybe he was too tired and busy to even notice me.

Was it my imagination, or did Eldest Brother move more awkwardly than usual? Normally he was very limber and climbed up the scaffolding easily and gracefully. That day, I caught my breath when I saw him slip once on the ladder. No question about it, he was already very tired, and the work day wasn't even half over.

I was afraid of disaster, and yet when the accident happened, it caught me by surprise. I heard a sudden cry, and then a thud as the electric saw Eldest Brother was using fell to the ground. He clutched his left hand tightly, and I saw bright-red blood flowing down his arm.

There were shouts and screams. I realized that the screams were coming from my own throat. Mr. Conner and a whole bunch of others rushed over to Eldest Brother. I seized the cyclone fence and shook it violently, trying to tear it down in my desperation to reach the other side.

Finally Mr. Conner opened the gate to the fence. He was supporting Eldest Brother as the two of them walked to his car. I rushed over to them. "How bad is it?" I cried.

"We'll have to get him to the hospital right away," said Mr. Conner. He helped Eldest Brother into the front seat. I couldn't see the injury, because somebody's flannel shirt was wrapped tightly around the hand. Already blood was oozing out and staining the shirt.

I got in the back seat and slammed the door a second before the car lurched into the road. Mr. Conner turned and said shortly, "The saw slipped and cut into his finger."

From the amount of blood, I guessed that the cut must have been a deep one. Did it sever the finger? Would Eldest Brother still be able to play the violin? That was the question that echoed over and over again in my mind as we raced for the hospital.

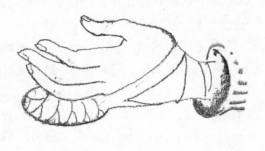

7

Mr. Conner and I had to stay in the waiting room while the doctor stitched Eldest Brother's finger. Mr. Conner's face was haggard. As he sat on the bench, he kept muttering to himself, "I shouldn't have done it! It's all my fault! If he loses that finger, I'll never forgive myself!"

I gathered he meant that he shouldn't have given Eldest Brother construction work. But it was too late for regrets. At least my worst nightmare hadn't come true: I had pictured Eldest Brother's finger completely cut off. If the doctor was stitching it, the finger must still be attached to the hand. But if there was nerve damage, he might not be able to play the violin again!

I had to tell my family the news. There was a phone just down the hall, and when Mother answered, I tried to think of a way to break it gently. But there was no gentle way to break news as bad as this. I took a deep breath. "Eldest Brother hurt his finger at work, and we're at Harborview Hospital," I told her.

Mother gasped. "How bad is it?"

"I don't know," I said. "The doctor is putting stitches in it. Maybe Mrs. Conner can give you a ride to the hospital."

Mother and Mrs. Conner arrived breathlessly fifteen minutes later. Mother was so disturbed that when she opened her mouth, her English deserted her completely.

"How did it happen, Mike?" Mrs. Conner asked her husband.

Mr. Conner groaned. "Oh, God, I don't know! I've asked myself that question over and over again! I wasn't there at the time, but according to one of the others, the saw just slipped in his hand, and then blood started to pour down."

"Was my son careless?" asked Mother. She had calmed down a bit and was able to speak English again.

"I would never have let him work if I thought he was the careless kind!" declared Mr. Conner. "But I had the feeling . . ." He hesitated.

I finished his thought. "Eldest Brother was already tired when he started work today, wasn't he?"

Mr. Conner nodded. "I saw he was kind of dragging himself along. The guy's been working too hard!"

So he had noticed it, too. Eldest Brother was strong. He could practice the violin furiously for hours at a time, but even he couldn't keep working two demanding jobs. It was exhaustion that had made his hand slip.

The door to the clinic room finally opened, and Eldest Brother walked out. His left hand was heavily bandaged and his face looked gray, but when he saw us he managed to smile. "It's not so bad!" he said quickly.

"J-j-just how bad?" whispered Mother.

"I cut the tendon of my fourth finger, but didn't damage the nerves," replied Eldest Brother. "Don't worry, it will heal in a couple of weeks. The nurse tells me I'll need some *rehab*, whatever that is."

I could feel the relief blow through all of us, like a gentle breeze. Mr. Conner took out a grungy piece of tissue and wiped his forehead. I took out an even grungier piece of tissue and wiped my eyes.

"Rehab means 'rehabilitation,'" said Mrs. Conner. "What the nurse means is that you have to do some special exercises to get that finger working properly again."

"In a just few weeks, you'll be able to do your fingering again," said Mother, smiling at Eldest Brother.

He managed to smile back. "I'll be able to carry a tray and wait tables in less time than that."

With his hand bandaged, Eldest Brother could not go back to work. He spent most of his time in his room. He couldn't even baby-sit, since he couldn't change a diaper with one hand. We were all touched when Peter Schultz came over with a bunch of pansies and a get-well card he had made himself. If you squinted, you could make out the shape of a violin in his drawing.

Eldest Brother moped around the house the whole time. At first I thought he was frustrated because he couldn't practice his violin. But when I asked him about it, all he would talk about was how much money he was losing every day he stayed away from work.

Two weeks after the accident, Eldest Brother

went back to the hospital to have the stitches taken out. I was shocked at the sight of his angry red scar, but at least he could play again.

"When are you going to start your rehab?" I asked him. "Did the nurse tell you what kind of exercises you have to do?"

"I have to flex my hand ten minutes a day," he said. "It's to prevent the finger from becoming stiff."

In his place, I would have immediately started doing the rehab exercises for twenty, thirty, forty minutes a day. But he seemed in no hurry to start. Didn't he see the danger? If the finger stiffened permanently, he might never be able to play properly again!

He was, however, in a hurry to start work again at the Sushi Hi. "Are you sure your hand is strong enough?" Mother asked him.

"Of course," Eldest Brother said quickly. "Besides, I need to start making money again."

"Shouldn't you at least wait until you've finished your rehab exercises?" I asked him. "Money isn't everything."

"It's good to be earning money!" said Eldest Brother. "You're always praising everything American. I should think that earning lots of money is exactly what American capitalism is all about!"

"Not all of our American friends are obsessed with making money!" I protested. "Look at the Conners. Matthew doesn't think about money all the time, nor do Mr. and Mrs. Conner!"

Eldest Brother wasn't ready to listen to preaching from a younger sister, and he didn't even bother to reply. He rushed out and I heard the front door slam.

I suddenly remembered the way he laughed and chatted with the other waiters at the restaurant. He looked like a normal teenage boy, happily earning good money and socializing with his friends. What's wrong with being a happy, normal teenage boy, anyway? Then my heart clenched when I thought of the gifted musician that Eldest Brother used to be.

As usual, I discussed my worries with Fourth Brother. He might not appreciate music, but he agreed that for Eldest Brother to stop playing the violin would be a tragic waste of talent.

Our favorite place for a private talk is in the basement. Fourth Brother will scratch a few notes, *di di di dah,* on his violin (the only time he touches his instrument, these days), and our cat,

Rita, will know this is a signal that we have a treat for her and she will come running.

I managed to save some tuna juice left in the can after Mother had scooped out the meat for our lunch. Then I soaked a small piece of bread in the juice. This is Rita's favorite treat.

After Rita had gulped down the treat, she carefully cleaned her paws. I stroked her silky fur and listened to her loud purr.

"How can we get Eldest Brother to do his rehab exercises so he can start playing the violin again?" I asked.

Fourth Brother crumpled a piece of paper into a ball, and Rita began to bat it around furiously. "He has to *want* to play," he said. "At the moment, he's so involved with earning money that he's forgetting what the money is for."

Making music is not a fast way to get rich. This is something our family has always known. We hear about superstars like Pincas Zukerman and Itzhak Perlman, who go around giving sold-out concerts and making heaps of money. Maybe Eldest Brother could become one of those superstars, maybe not. Most musicians are like Father, making enough to support a family, but not expecting to get really rich. Father, Mother, Second Sister, and I have all accepted this. We make music our career because that's what we love more than anything else in the world. Until now, Eldest Brother did, too.

After talking things over, Fourth Brother and I finally decided that another visit to Mr. Vitelli would steer Eldest Brother back toward music.

I told Eldest Brother that I needed a new C-string for my cello and persuaded him to come with me to Mr. Vitelli's shop. That turned out to be a disastrous mistake.

8

"So how is that buzzing in your violin?" Mr. Vitelli asked Eldest Brother when we arrived.

"Not getting any better," replied Eldest Brother.

Mr. Vitelli and I waited. We were both expecting Eldest Brother to bring up the subject of renting a violin. Instead, he walked over to the shelf of new instruments. "Where is that violin you finished making last month?" he suddenly exclaimed.

"I sold it two weeks ago," said Mr. Vitelli, and sighed. He added sadly, "You know, I had hoped at first that *you* might find some way to buy it."

There was a long silence. I couldn't bear to look at Eldest Brother, to see his bitter disappointment. When I finally lifted my eyes to his face, I saw that it was set like stone.

"I just couldn't turn down this offer," said Mr. Vitelli. He sounded defensive. "The first violinist of the River Quartet was in town, and when he saw this violin, he immediately wanted to buy it."

There was another long silence. Mr. Vitelli cleared his throat. "It's good for my reputation, you know, when someone like that buys an instrument from me."

I had heard of the River Quartet and had even gone to one of their concerts. They were a young quartet, formed only three years ago, but they were already famous all over the country. The first violinist had a lovely singing tone, and I could imagine how gorgeous Mr. Vitelli's instrument would sound in his hands.

I paid for my cello string, and the two of us walked slowly out of the shop. At the bus stop, I cleared my throat. "It's not the end of the world. Mr. Vitelli can make another violin just as good. Maybe even better!"

"It's the best violin he will ever make," Eldest Brother said softly. "And he knows it."

There was nothing to say. In my heart I knew he was right.

Now that Eldest Brother had no hope of buying the violin he had set his heart on, I would have thought that earning money would be less important to him.

But he went off to the Sushi Hi, and when he returned home, he counted his earnings just as eagerly as before.

"What are you going to do with all this money you saved?" I asked him. "Even though you can't buy Mr. Vitelli's violin, you have more than enough to rent a good one."

He turned on me savagely. "Stop nagging me! I'm sick and tired of hearing you go on and on about renting a violin!"

In the weeks that followed, Eldest Brother seemed to have lost interest in music. When some of Father's fellow musicians came over to play quartets and trios, Eldest Brother didn't even go downstairs and listen.

What if he decided to give up music entirely? He might want to become a full-time carpenter instead, like Mr. Conner. Or he might open up a restaurant, make polyester shingles, sell felt tents and silk parkas... On that thought, I wanted to cry.

* * *

I thought about what Fourth Brother had said: Eldest Brother had to *want* to play again. The way things were going, it didn't seem like he ever would. "It's time for us to think up a plan," I said to Fourth Brother.

Fourth Brother had an idea. "I'll get Matthew to come over and play for Eldest Brother. Maybe when he sees how beautifully Matthew plays, Eldest Brother might get back his own love for music."

I liked his idea, but I added a twist. "Let's ask Matthew to play a piece that's way too hard for him. Then Eldest Brother will have to pick up his violin to help."

Matthew was eager to be part of the plan. He also missed playing in our family quartet. He came over that night with his fiddle and asked which piece he should play. I handed him the music for a Bach unaccompanied partita. It was one of Eldest Brother's favorite pieces, and it was much too hard for Matthew.

When Matthew saw the music, he yelped. "I can't do that piece! I'd *murder* it!"

"That's exactly what we want you to do," I told him. We convinced him that it was for a good cause.

So Matthew, Fourth Brother, and I trooped

into Eldest Brother's room. We found him lying in bed, looking at the ceiling. His pay stubs were stacked in a neat pile on his desk next to a calculator. His violin was nowhere to be seen. "What do you want?" he snapped.

Matthew cleared his throat. "I'm planning to audition for the All-City Orchestra this fall, and I'm thinking of playing a movement of this. What do you think?"

He held out the sheet music. After a few seconds, Eldest Brother heaved himself up and glanced at the music. Then he looked more closely. "It's the gigue from the E Major Partita! You're thinking of playing *that*?"

"I thought I'd impress the conductor," Matthew said. "The problem is, there are some passages that don't sound quite right."

Eldest Brother raised his eyebrows. "I'm not surprised! All right, let's hear you play."

Matthew took out his fiddle, tuned it quickly, and swallowed hard. Then he plunged in. You had to give him credit for guts — or gall. Anyway, some part of his innards. He struggled heroically, but there were just too many flying notes for him.

Even Fourth Brother knew that things were not going well. Matthew's sweating brow and

tightly clenched teeth told the whole story. At the end, Matthew lowered his fiddle and hung his head.

There was a long silence. Then Matthew looked up. "I think I need some help with those double and triple stops," he admitted.

Another long silence. I felt a hysterical urge to laugh, but managed to fight it down. Finally Eldest Brother got up from the bed, walked over to Matthew, and took the violin gently from his hands. "You need help with a few other things, too," he said.

He picked up Matthew's bow and started to play. After a couple of measures, he suddenly winced, and the bow screeched across the string. He put the instrument down and lay back down on his bed.

"Maybe I should play an easier piece, huh?" asked Matthew. He took out another piece of music, the one he had really intended to play for the audition.

It was the "Meditation" from *Thaïs*, by Massenet, a short work and not very showy, but very lyrical. Matthew closed his eyes and began to play. He had obviously practiced hard on the piece, and he went into it without having to worry about the notes. We had all known for some time that Matthew was talented, so I was not surprised at the musicianship he showed. But I was still overwhelmed by the beauty that poured out of his instrument and flooded the small room.

Matthew played his heart out. He fully understood the importance of what he was doing. Eldest Brother's recovery meant almost as much to him as it did to our family.

I felt my eyes fill with tears. I glanced at Eldest Brother and saw that tears were rolling down his cheeks. Our plan had worked.

Eldest Brother started his rehab exercises that very night. I could tell it was painful, but he kept it up for the full ten minutes. The following day he did it for fifteen minutes.

By the end of the summer, he was exercising his finger twenty minutes a day, and it seemed to be doing well. He went back to waiting tables at the Sushi Hi, but worked only a few days a week. When school started in the fall, he worked there only on weekends. He still babysat the Schultzes once in a while, because Peter asked for him. But he had lost his feverish desire to earn money.

He decided to rent a violin. It was not the one he had fallen in love with, but it was a good one. Mr. Vitelli told him that the rent could go toward the purchase price, if he wanted. When I asked Eldest Brother what that meant, he said that if he had enough money to buy the instrument someday, the amount of rent he had already paid could be taken off the price. I thought this was pretty decent of Mr. Vitelli.

I was so relieved that Eldest Brother started to play again. To me, he sounded almost as good as he used to, but he said he had a long way to go before full recovery.

Although Eldest Brother was now playing regularly, he seemed to have lost his passion. I had the feeling that a dream had been shattered when Mr. Vitelli's lovely violin was lost to him. The instrument had been a target, something to aim for. Now it was gone forever.

I could tell that Father was as disturbed as I was about Eldest Brother's playing. Father had known that he himself was an able musician, someone who could get a job with a good orchestra and maybe work himself into the first chair, or at least the second. But he knew he would never be a superstar, someone who would play the solo part of a violin concerto in major concert halls across the country.

All his hopes had been concentrated on Eldest Brother. If anyone in our family had a chance of becoming a great soloist, it was Eldest Brother. He had the will, the fire, and the brilliance. At least he used to.

I went back to listening to the two of them play duets in the living room. The first time they played together again, Eldest Brother said to Father, "My finger still isn't quite good enough. I'll take the easier part."

Never before had Eldest Brother asked to take an easier part. He had always rushed into the hardest thing he could manage. What had happened to him? I remembered the confident way he had climbed trees and the easy way he had moved around the house frames while working with Mr. Conner. He had lost that confidence when he dropped the saw and cut his finger.

I saw on Father's face the same shock that I felt. "No, no!" he said. "You take the top part, as usual. I don't mind if you slip up now and then. Things will get better."

But Eldest Brother insisted on playing the

lower part. The duet sounded wretched, because Father didn't play as well as he usually did, either.

I went up to Father at the end of the session, after Eldest Brother had gone upstairs. "He's lost his self-confidence, hasn't he?" I said softly.

Father tried to hide his despair. "I guess we'll just have to give him more time."

"Maybe what he needs is something to aim for," I said.

But what? What could we do to put the brilliance back into Eldest Brother's playing?

Then a week later, Father came home with shining eyes. "I've got wonderful news!"

He refused to tell us the news until the whole family was gathered around the table at dinner. "I heard that one of our local software billionaires is trying to find some way to spend his money," he began.

That wasn't news. There are a number of superrich computer moguls in Seattle who spend their money on various projects, both public and private. They usually involve buildings, very large buildings. So what was wonderful about that? We looked blankly at Father.

"This man has a really original idea," continued Father. "He's bought a Stradivarius violin, and he plans to hold an annual audition for young local musicians. The winner gets to play the instrument for six months and then perform in a special recital!"

We all gasped. Antonio Stradivari was a famous Italian violin maker, and a Stradivarius is an instrument made by him or a member of his family. Even today, nobody knows what the secret of his success was, and there are all sorts of wild theories. Some say it was the varnish he used; some say it was the water in the local river that he soaked the wood in. Whatever it was, people still think that no modern violin is as good as a Stradivarius. I had heard that a Stradivarius violin was recently auctioned off for more than two million dollars! It's the dream of every string player to hold a genuine Stradivarius in his hands. To be able to play it for six whole months! Wow! It was an intoxicating thought.

One by one, we all turned to look at Eldest Brother.

I saw his face light up with joy, but it lasted only a moment. Then his smile faded and he looked down at his rice bowl.

"Well?" said Father. "What do you say, Yingwu?"

Eldest Brother toyed with his chopsticks, and

then put them down and looked at his hands. "What's the use? With my weak finger, I'll just make a fool of myself."

"You don't have to audition this year, or even next year," said Father, refusing to give up. "But your finger will recover completely, and then you can give it a try. It's something to aim for, one day."

Eldest Brother didn't reply. His face was frozen in despair. I opened my mouth to argue with him, but I saw Mother shaking her head sadly. I looked around the table and saw sorrow on every face. Father's anguish was the worst, because he had had the highest hopes.

9

"Father's fortieth birthday is next month," said Second Sister. "It's a big birthday. Let's get together and buy him something really special."

"All right," I said. "What shall we get him?"

We had a lot of money, if we pooled together the baby-sitting money Second Sister and I had, plus Fourth Brother's money from delivering newspapers. Eldest Brother had the most money, but we didn't want to ask him to contribute too much, since he still had to save to buy his violin.

The trouble was that we couldn't think what we should buy. We consulted Mother, and she couldn't think of anything, either. None of our friends were very helpful.

"A tie," said Kim. "That's what kids always buy for their dad's birthday."

"My father hates ties," I told her. "He owns exactly one tie, which he wears for everything. Besides, this is an important birthday, and we want to get him something really nice."

"A season ticket to the Mariners games," suggested Paul. Being an avid baseball player and fan, it's what he himself wished for. But my father doesn't know a thing about baseball. He still refers to batting as "swishing that stick in the air."

"Some CDs or sheet music," suggested Matthew. That was a much better present for a man whose life revolved around the violin.

Fourth Brother came up with the best idea. "How about organizing a surprise concert for him? We can invite some of his friends in the orchestra and have them play one of his favorite pieces."

Second Sister smiled at him. "I like that! It's much better than buying him something. He doesn't care for material things."

Eldest Brother didn't have any suggestions because he was at work at the Sushi Hi. But it was the thought of Eldest Brother that gave me my inspiration. I thought of a present that would please Father more than anything else in the world.

"Instead of having Father's friends play for him, let's play something *ourselves*," I suggested. "How about picking a string quartet with an especially dazzling part for Eldest Brother?"

The others saw what I was driving at, and I could see from their smiles that they all thought it was great idea. I was pretty proud of it myself.

We discussed which quartet to play. We couldn't pick anything too hard, since Matthew was playing the second violin part. While he is really gifted musically, he hasn't been playing as long as the rest of us, so he couldn't manage anything too demanding — like that Bach partita we forced him to play. We finally chose Haydn's Lark Quartet. It's one of Father's favorites, and the first violin part, Eldest Brother's, has some brilliant passages.

The only thing that made me feel bad was the thought of Fourth Brother. He had given up his second violin position to his friend Matthew, so he would have no part in the performance. It's not that I was sorry he wasn't playing the violin anymore, but I didn't like the thought that he would be left out of the birthday present.

But Fourth Brother was cheerful about it. "Don't worry about me, Third Sister. In fact, I've already thought of something I *can* contribute."

I didn't know whether he was telling the truth or just trying to make me feel better. He wouldn't tell me what his plan was. "I want it to be a surprise," he said.

When Eldest Brother came home that night, we told him about our idea for Father's present. He looked at me for a long moment. Finally he gave a wry grin. "You can't fool me. I know what you're up to. But have you thought of what would happen if I can't play the first violin part properly? My finger still hurts when I stretch it. It would be a pretty shabby present for Father if I messed up the part."

"You won't mess it up," I said, with more confidence than I felt.

At least Eldest Brother agreed to practice the part. In fact, practicing was our problem, since we couldn't do it when Father was around. Finally Mr. and Mrs. Conner offered to let us play at their house whenever Father was home in the evenings. After a couple of weeks, Father began to complain that his children kept disappearing from the house right after dinner.

Fortunately Father's birthday fell on a day when he was not playing with the Seattle Symphony. The Engs had invited us to their house for dinner that night. Father looked a little hurt when Mother nonchalantly told him about the invitation. Of course, it was a treat to have dinner with the Engs — Mrs. Eng and her daughter, Melanie, are wonderful cooks — but I could tell that Father had been counting on a special family party to observe his birthday.

One by one, we younger Yangs went to the Engs before our parents, and we let Mother think up reasons to tell Father. I had a feeling that Father suspected something was up, but I was still sure our concert would be a complete surprise.

When we arrived at the Engs, we changed into our concert costumes. Second Sister and I were dressed alike in elegant white blouses and black skirts. "I've never spent this much money before on a blouse!" Second Sister had grumbled when she and I went out shopping for the clothes.

"We have to look professional," I said. I wanted us to look like real, professional musicians. It was a declaration to Father that we were serious about music, and it was an essential part of our present to him. Eldest Brother put on his dark gray suit, the one he wore for playing in public, and even Matthew wore a suit his father had rented for him.

The Engs got the house all ready for the big party. They were delighted to join our plot and went to a lot of trouble to set up rows of chairs for the recital. They also ordered a huge birthday cake.

Mother provided most of the other food for the dinner, which consisted mainly of huge platters of stir-fried noodles. Noodles are served at a Chinese birthday party, since the long strands mean a long life for the guest of honor. To make things simpler, Mother had brought over the food earlier in the day, and Mrs. Eng had offered to heat it up before serving.

We finished setting up our stands just before the guests arrived. In addition to some of our friends, many of Father's students and their families came. It was beginning to look like a student recital, except that we Yangs would provide the only music.

It was the music I was anxious about. The previous night, Second Sister and I had talked softly in our room as we were getting ready for bed. "What do you think of Eldest Brother's playing?" I asked.

Second Sister finished buttoning her pajama top before she answered. "He got all the right notes," she said slowly. "They were not easy notes, either."

I waited, but she didn't say anything more. I climbed into bed and drew the covers up to my neck. "I thought his playing was . . . well —" I stopped, finding it hard to go on. Finally I swallowed. "He didn't play with his old brilliance."

Second Sister pulled the covers over her face. When she spoke her voice was muffled, and what I thought she said was, "Stop talking and let me sleep."

Now, as I watched the guests coming through the front door of the Engs' chatting and laughing, I tried to hide my anxiety. Eldest Brother was talking to the Schultz family, and he smiled at something Peter was saying. At least he did not look worried.

Mr. and Mrs. Conner came up to talk to Eldest Brother, and Mr. Conner's face showed a trace of worry. I knew it wasn't for Matthew.

Where was Fourth Brother? I still felt sorry that he had no part in the music for Father's birthday. I looked around and finally saw him in the front hall, greeting the guests. Not only that, he was passing out sheets of paper to everyone.

I walked up and took one of the sheets. It was printed with the following:

In Honor of
Xinyu Yang's
40th Birthday
A Special Performance of
The String Quartet in D Major,
Op. 64, no. 5, "The Lark"
By Franz Joseph Haydn
Allegro Moderato
Adagio — Cantabile
Minuetto: Allegretto
Finale: Vivace
Performers:
First Violin — Yingwu Yang
Second Violin — Matthew Conner
Viola — Yinglan Yang
Violincello — Yingmei Yang

On the back was the same thing, but translated into Chinese.

I was delighted. "How did you do this?" I asked Fourth Brother.

He grinned, looking very pleased. "Mr. Eng told me about a printing shop in Chinatown that does both Chinese and English."

Second Sister and Eldest Brother each came up and grabbed a program. Eldest Brother looked at his program for a long time, then

folded it carefully and put it in his pocket.

"It must have cost a lot of money to print this!" said Second Sister. She looked especially impressed by the Chinese side.

"He saved up for it," said Matthew. "I gave him my paper route, so he could earn more money."

When word got around that Fourth Brother

was the one who had the programs printed, he received so many compliments that he began to look embarrassed. At last, he was saved by the bell (another one of my favorite expressions).

Mrs. Eng, who had been peeking out the front window, shushed everyone. "Here they come!"

The bell rang, and Mr. Eng went to open the door. My parents came into the house and were greeted by the quartet and the guests breaking out into "Happy Birthday to You!"

Stunned, Father stood frozen by the door and had to be prodded forward by Mother. He was still dazed when Fourth Brother handed him a program and ushered him to the seat of honor in the middle of the front row. He looked down at the program and finally understood what his birthday present was.

As we picked up our instruments, I stole a look at Father. I saw the expressions pass over his face: first radiant hope, and then agonizing fear. That was when I saw what a terrible risk our concert was. If Eldest Brother played badly, or even indifferently, this public disgrace would completely crush him. He might never play another note in his life.

I began to feel dizzy. In my anxiety, I had forgotten to breathe. Then I took a deep breath and we began to play.

The first movement of the quartet opened with just the three lower strings playing short, choppy notes. In the eighth measure, it was time for the entrance of the first violin. Eldest Brother closed his eyes, hesitated just a tiny fraction of a second, and then launched into his brilliant solo.

Suddenly I realized that this wasn't about Mr. Vitelli's violin. Even the Stradivarius wasn't so important. What really mattered was that Eldest Brother had rediscovered the joy of making music.

I heard his notes soar up, like a lark flying off into the sky.